Pete the Cat
and the Easter Basket Bandit

by Kimberly & James Dean

HARPER FESTIVAL
An Imprint of HarperCollinsPublishers

ISBN 978-0-06-286837-4

The artist used pen and ink, with watercolor and acrylic paint, on
300lb hot press paper to create the illustrations for this book

22 23 24 25 26 IMG 10 9 8 7 6 5 4 3 2 1
❖
First Edition

One Easter morning, Pete the Cat discovers his Easter basket is missing!

"Where is my Easter basket?" he asks.

Pete looks everywhere.
It's not here.

Or there.

It's not anywhere!

Then Pete spots a bright blue dot on the floor.

It's a jelly bean, Pete's favorite! Pete finds another. Then another. And another. It's a whole trail of colorful jelly beans.

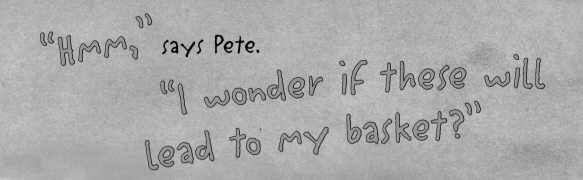

"Hmm," says Pete. "I wonder if these will lead to my basket?"

Pete follows the jelly beans down the street and around the corner to . . .

Callie's house!

"Callie, have you seen my Easter basket?" Pete asks.

"No," says Callie, "but I see a trail of candy eggs."

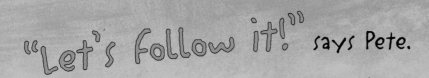

"Let's follow it!" says Pete.

Pete and Callie follow the candy eggs
through the yard and across a field to . . .

Alligator's house!
"Alligator, have you seen Pete's Easter basket?" asks Callie.

"I haven't," says Alligator, "but look at this
trail of marshmallow chicks."

"We should see where it goes!" says Pete.

Pete and Callie and Alligator follow the marshmallow chicks around the pond to . . .

Gus's house!

"Gus, have you seen Pete's Easter basket?"
asks Alligator.

"It's not here," says Gus, "but there are all these
lollipops on the ground."

"It's a lollipop trail," says Callie. "Let's follow it!"

So Pete and Callie and Alligator and Gus follow the lollipops out the door and up the path to . . .

Turtle's house!

"Turtle, have you seen Pete's Easter basket?" asks Gus.

"No," says Turtle, "but look! There are a bunch of chocolate bunnies leading that way."

Pete and Callie and Alligator and Gus and Turtle
follow the chocolate bunny trail to the playground.

It goes under the swings and down the slide
and around the monkey bars to a colorful little
house in the garden.

"It looks like the trail ends here,"
says Turtle.

But before Pete can knock, the door swings open and everyone gasps!

It's the Easter Bunny!

"Easter Bunny, have you seen my Easter basket?" asks Pete.
The Easter Bunny looks sad.

"Yes," he says. "I have it. Every year I deliver all the Easter baskets, but I never get one of my own. So I borrowed yours."

The Easter Bunny sniffles. "I was going to bring it back soon. I'm very sorry, Pete."

Pete smiles and hugs the Easter Bunny.

"That's okay," says Pete. "I understand."

Then Pete has a great idea. He puts some of his candy in an empty basket. He asks Callie and Alligator and Gus and Turtle to all add candy from their baskets, too. Soon the new basket is bursting with treats.

Pete hands the basket to the Easter Bunny.

"Happy Easter!" Pete says. "This one is just for you."

The Easter Bunny is so happy!
"Thank you so much, everyone!" he says,
and gleefully eats a jelly bean from
his first ever Easter basket.

Pete and his friends promise to make the Easter Bunny a basket every year from now on.

Sharing is the sweetest gift of all.